THE
FORGOTTEN
GROVE OF FIRE

SAM & SOFIA'S
SCOOTER STORIES

Written by Colton Mooney

Illustrated by Rhiannon Davenport

First paperback edition printed in 2024 by Little Passports, Inc.
Copyright © 2024 Conscious Content Media, Inc.
All rights reserved.

Written by Colton Mooney
Interior Illustrations by Rhiannon Davenport
Cover Illustration by Jane Pica

Printed in China, Shenzhen
10 9 8 7 6 5 4 3 2 1

Little Passports, Inc.
121 Varick Street, Floor 3
New York, NY 10013
www.LittlePassports.com
ISBN: 978-1-953148-19-3

Contents

1

An Unexpected Friend

Sam was about to plant his next flower seed when he heard Sofia shout, "Heads up!" He turned around just in time to dodge a spray of water.

"Sorry!" Sofia said, leaning over to wipe some drips from his arm.

"That was a close one," Sam said, pushing his brown hair from his eyes.

"Nice reflexes," said Sofia, turning back to the flowerpots in front of her. "This nozzle's a little tricky." She carefully squeezed the handle of the garden hose in her hands, lightly misting the soil in the pots.

"I didn't realize I'd need an umbrella today," Sam said.

The two friends shared a laugh in the flower bed of Aunt Charlie's garden. Sofia crouched low with the hose while Sam knelt next to her in front of a rectangular planter, his hands flecked with dirt. Behind them, the house Sam shared with his aunt stood framed by the soft colors of dusk.

Aunt Charlie had just returned from a work trip exploring the flora of Canada's Yukon territory. She'd arrived that morning and had barely dropped her bags before showing Sam and

Sofia her photos, videos, field notes, and even clippings of some of Canada's most interesting flowers. During his aunt's trip, Sam had stayed with Sofia and her parents, Mama Lyla and Papai Luiz. While Sam was there, Mama Lyla had shown him how to use her garden tools, so the minute

he saw the seeds Aunt Charlie had brought home, he eagerly asked if he and Sofia could start planting.

Now Sam looked down at the flower bed, his best

friend Sofia beside him and the pleasant smell of moist earth filling his nostrils. He carefully opened a paper packet and sprinkled a few brown seeds into the shallow hole he'd dug, then scooped soil on top and gently pressed it into place.

"Perfect!" said Sofia.

"I didn't pack the soil too tightly?" Sam asked.

Sofia shook her head. "Nope. You planted the seeds exactly the way Aunt Charlie told us to."

Right on cue, Aunt Charlie's voice floated toward them from across the yard. "How's it coming along?" She walked over with a tray of frosty glasses and some soda bottles.

"Great!" Sofia answered.

"I'm almost done with my first row of seeds," Sam said.

"Terrific!" Aunt Charlie joined them, sitting cross-legged on the ground. She rested her tray on one of Sofia's empty pots. "You two thirsty?"

Sofia's eyes lit up at the sight of the glasses covered in condensation. "I am now," she said.

Aunt Charlie passed each of them a glass and took the third for herself. "I brought maple syrup soda back from my trip," she said. "Seemed like the perfect treat for planting Canadian flowers."

Sam raised the glass to his lips and took a sip. The sweet flavor tingled over his tongue in a fizz of bubbles. "Wow, that's delicious!"

Sofia smiled and nodded her agreement.

Aunt Charlie took a sip, then turned to the flower bed.

"Which flower did you start with, Sam?"

Sam lifted the photo he'd pulled from Aunt Charlie's notes. It showed a cluster of small pinkish-purple flowers growing close to the ground.

"Purple saxifrage," Sam said. "They're one of my favorites from your photos."

"And they look even better in person," Aunt Charlie said.

"How long will they take to grow?" Sofia asked.

"It'll be a week or two before they sprout," Aunt Charlie said. She leaned forward to inspect Sam's work. "Smart to plant them at the edge of the flower bed. They'll stay close to the ground, and we can plant taller flowers behind them. They like cooler conditions, too, so it's good they're in the shade."

"It's kind of funny," Sofia said, "Sam chose the shady flowers, and I chose the opposite."

"What do you mean?" Aunt Charlie asked.

Sofia turned on her knees and grabbed a pot from behind her, holding it up. "Sunflowers!" she said. A few small stalks stood proudly in the pot's soil, each supporting a flower head surrounded by green leaves growing outward on thin stems. The pointed petals created bright yellow halos around the flowers' dark centers.

"Okanagan sunflowers, to be exact," Aunt Charlie said, lifting Sofia's pot. "Before we got to the Yukon, we stopped in a city called Kelowna. I took these clippings from a hillside. They were growing everywhere!" She gave the flowers a sniff. "The indigenous Inuit people of Canada once relied on this plant as a food source, and today it's considered a symbol of Kelowna."

Sam imagined hills and hills full of yellow sunflower blossoms. "Can you take clippings from all flowers?"

"Not all plants grow well from clippings," Aunt Charlie said. "Some plant roots need soil to grow. Sunflowers can actually be hard to transport because their petals are so delicate, but we wrapped these really carefully." She tucked a strand of her red hair behind her ear and handed the pot back to Sofia. "And it's important to take clippings responsibly," she added. "Local gardeners invited us to clip these sunflowers, and in the Yukon, we were given permission by the botanical society overseeing the land we were visiting. Earth's creations are precious, so we have to protect them while we learn about them."

"I can't wait to watch them grow," Sam said, adding more purple saxifrage seeds to another hole in the ground.

"Me too," Aunt Charlie said, taking a sip of soda. "They'll be our own little slice of Canada in the garden."

"What was your favorite flower from the trip, Aunt Charlie?" Sofia asked.

"Well," said Aunt Charlie, lowering her glass,

"I didn't get to see my *favorite* flower. It's purple, and it grows in tall feathery stalks. It's called fireweed and it grows wild in the Yukon."

Sam recognized the name from Aunt Charlie's notes. He flipped through some pages until he found what he was looking for. "Are you

talking about *Chamaenerion angustifolium*?"

"Yes," said Aunt Charlie. "That's its scientific name."

"You didn't find any?" Sam asked.

"Unfortunately, no," Aunt Charlie answered. "But never fear! We found plenty of other wonderful specimens."

"Maybe you'll find fireweed next time," Sofia said hopefully.

"Precisely!" Aunt Charlie said, raising her glass. "There's always next time. In fact, I'm already planning another trip for next year. I can't resist! You know how much I love a good expedition. Besides, a love of adventure runs in the family," she added, nodding at Sam.

"That reminds me," Aunt Charlie said, pulling a small tablet from her shirt pocket. "We met some wonderful people on our trip, including someone I want to introduce you to."

She tapped the tablet a few times, then turned the screen toward Sam and Sofia. They leaned close and watched as Aunt Charlie played the video. A girl about Sam and Sofia's age stepped onto the screen and waved, dimples appearing in her cheeks as she smiled.

"Hi, Sam!" she said. "Hi, Sofia! I'm Amka. We've been showing the scientists some of our favorite spots." Sam smiled as he noticed the sunflower tucked into Amka's dark hair, which was pulled back into a long ponytail. "I've been coming to these trails here in the Yukon since I was little,"

Amka continued. She motioned to the pathway behind her, which was framed by shrubs, small trees, and pops of colorful flowers. "There are a lot of natural treasures here in Canada."

"Tons!" Aunt Charlie said, her face dipping into the video frame for a moment.

Amka giggled in response, then turned back to the camera. "Maybe next time you two can come along and explore for yourselves. *Tavvauvusi!*" Amka gave another wave, and the video stopped.

"That was nice of her to say hello," Sofia said.

"She was a great guide too," Aunt Charlie said, tucking the tablet back into her pocket.

"What did she say at the end?" asked Sofia.

"*Tavvauvusi*," Aunt Charlie repeated. "It's one of the Inuktitut words for 'goodbye.' "

"How'd you meet Amka?" Sam asked.

"I've known her grandmother Adjiukak for years," Aunt Charlie said. "When we were looking for some extra help identifying local flowers, Adjiukak suggested Amka. She came along on a few of our field surveys, and she gave me the seeds you're planting, Sam."

"Really?!" Sam asked.

Aunt Charlie nodded.

Sam imagined himself on the path from Amka's video, taking photo after photo of the beautiful landscape. He was lost in thought until motion at the corner of his eye caught his attention. Sam turned to see a black cat padding along the fence at the edge of the yard.

"Amka gave me something else," Aunt Charlie said. From another pocket, Aunt Charlie pulled out an envelope and handed it to Sam.

"A letter?" Sam asked, taking the envelope.

"I thought you two might want to be her pen pals," Aunt Charlie said.

"Yes, we're always looking for new pen pals!" Sofia said.

"Great!" Aunt Charlie stood, brushing off her legs. "I'm going to keep sorting my files from the trip. Let me know if you need anything."

Sam opened the envelope as Aunt Charlie walked back to the house. He pulled out the letter and unfolded it so Sofia could read with him.

Hi Sam and Sofia!

Your aunt said you might want to be pen pals, so here I am writing our first letter. To start things off, I thought I'd tell you a story. It's an old family folktale my grandmother has been telling me for as long as I can remember.

According to our ancestors, there is a mystical place called the Forgotten Grove of Fire hidden somewhere in the mountains of Canada. The grove is said to bring visitors peace, inspiration, and good luck. No one knows exactly where it is, but three clues have been passed down through generations:

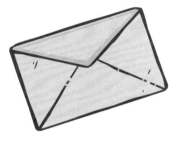

Follow the purple footprints from the mouth of the bear.

The path will be hidden beyond the Emerald Door, an entrance next to the farthest-reaching hand and visible only by the strongest light.

There lie the green flames that sing the sky's song: the Forgotten Grove of Fire.

I wish I could look for the grove, but my grandma says it's probably in Canada's Northwest Territory, much too far from where I live in Whitehorse. I'd *go hunting for it if I had a way to get there!*

Hope you're having a great time in Compass Court.

Your new pen pal (I hope!),

Amka

Sam lowered the letter, excitement building in his chest. He looked at Sofia, who was smiling from ear to ear.

"Amka wishes she had a way to hunt for the grove," Sam said.

"And *we* happen to have a way," Sofia said.

"There's still time before sunset," Sam said. "Are you thinking what I'm thinking?"

Meow! Sam turned to see the black cat watching them from the fence.

Sofia giggled. "It sounds like the cat is thinking it too."

"Let's go!" Sam said.

The pair tucked away their gardening tools, brushed the dirt from their clothes, finished

their maple sodas, and ran around the side of the house. When they reached the side door to the garage, Sam turned the handle, stepped inside, and turned on the light to illuminate Aunt Charlie's lab.

The room was full of tools, inventions, and gadgets, and its shelves were packed with supplies for various projects. But what Sam and Sofia needed wasn't on any shelf. Across the room, in the corner, something big and bulky was covered by a tarp. Sam grabbed the corner of the fabric and pulled. The covering fell away to reveal a ruby-red scooter. The amazing invention, programmed with special teleportation technology created by Aunt Charlie, had already taken Sam and Sofia on many whirlwind trips across the world. Sam wasn't sure if Aunt Charlie knew about their global adventures, but she'd shown him the scooter for a reason, hadn't she? And how could they resist making a new friend *and* hunting for the Forgotten Grove of Fire?

Sam hopped on the scooter and Sofia climbed up behind him. He tapped the touch screen anchored between the handlebars, looked at Amka's envelope, and entered the name of her hometown.

"Ready?" Sam asked over his shoulder.

"*Vamos!*" Sofia said.

Sam tapped the button on the screen, its pulsing glow like an invitation. The scooter rumbled to life beneath them, surrounding the two friends in an orb of bright, swirling light. Sam squeezed his eyes closed.

Whiz . . . Zoom . . . FOOP!

2

The Winning Goal

No matter how many times the scooter whizzed Sam and Sofia across the world, Sam never got completely used to the sensation. He clung tightly to the handlebars until the engine quieted beneath him, and when he opened his eyes the scooter's lights were dimming. He blinked a few times and looked around.

The scooter had appeared on a quiet street lined with houses, some of them painted warm oranges and reds and others vibrant greens and purples. Off in the distance, Sam could see the glittering water of a large lake, and above them, the vast sky stretched far and wide in a beautiful clear blue. He took a breath, enjoying the refreshing chill in the air.

"We're in Canada!" Sofia said from behind Sam.

Sam looked at the scooter's touch screen. "The city of Whitehorse, to be exact."

"Whoa," Sofia said. "It seems like the sky never ends."

"Looks like we're a few blocks from Amka's house," Sam said. He entered the address from Amka's envelope and started up the scooter as Sofia pulled helmets from the compartment under the seat. The screen brought up directions, and with a twist of the handlebars, they were zipping down the road.

Cars drove alongside as Sam directed the scooter through town. They passed a few people walking past rows of markets, cafés, and more colorful houses. After another block, they were turning onto Amka's street, and they didn't have to look hard to find her.

In the middle of the quiet road, a group of kids were zipping back and forth on inline skates, laughing and shouting while they tapped and swung what looked like long sticks. As the scooter approached, the group dispersed, rolling out of the street to make room.

"Nice scooter!" a voice called as Sam brought their ride to a stop.

"Thanks!" Sofia said.

"We're looking for Amka," Sam said, and just as the words escaped his mouth, he saw her.

She skated over, pulling off her helmet to reveal her long hair. "That's me," she said, dimples puckering her cheeks.

Sam parked the scooter and stepped off. "I'm Sam," he said. "This is Sofia." Sofia hopped off and gave a wave. "Sorry for showing up unannounced," he continued, "but my aunt—"

"Aunt Charlie!" Amka said. "She gave you the letter I wrote."

Sofia nodded. "And your video."

"I can't believe you're on my street," said Amka as the other kids gathered around. "How'd you get here?"

"It's kind of a long story," Sam said.

"I love stories!" Amka said. "You can tell me after the game."

"Are you playing hockey?" Sofia asked.

"You know it," one of the kids answered.

"Street hockey," said another.

"Want to join?" asked Amka.

Sam looked at Sofia, who nodded with a smile. "Let's do it!" she said.

A tall boy wearing a green bandanna on his head waved them over. "We were missing two players anyway," he said. "This is perfect. I'm Scott, by the way." He pulled a couple pairs of inline skates from a big plastic bin. "Let me know if these don't fit."

"Do you know how to skate?" Amka asked Sam and Sofia.

Sam took the skates from Scott. "We can ice skate," he said. "Is street skating the same?"

"Sort of," Scott answered, bending to stretch his long legs.

"I've always wanted to learn how to play hockey," Sofia said, strapping on the inline skates before gliding over to Scott and Amka.

Sam was nervous he wouldn't pick up on the skating as fast as Sofia, but his skates gripped the rough road and gave him traction. He felt more in control than he had expected.

After tightening the straps of their scooter helmets and each taking a long wooden hockey stick, Sam and Sofia were ready for Amka to tell them what to do.

"The trick is to use the hockey stick like it's an extension of your arm," she said. "You don't just want to fling the stick around and slap at the hockey puck. Let it move with you." She moved her stick back and forth to demonstrate, Sam and Sofia mirroring her.

"Just like that," said Amka. "You can also use the stick to steady yourself and balance."

Sam skated back and forth a few times, adjusting the hockey stick each time he wobbled.

"Looking good!" Scott called. He adjusted his bandanna and skated to the other side of the street. "You ready?"

Amka smiled at Sam and Sofia, and they all nodded at Scott.

Sam joined Amka's team, while Sofia joined Scott's. Amka placed the puck in the center of the makeshift ring. "We're tied right now," she said, joining Sam and the rest of their team. "Whoever scores the next point wins the game, okay?"

Sam nodded and saw Sofia do the same across the road.

One of the kids blew a whistle, and they were off.

Everyone skated toward the puck. Scott reached it first and pushed it along with his stick. He rolled forward a few strides and passed it back to Sofia, who spun past another player and started working her way toward the goal behind Sam.

Sam followed her as she pulled her stick back and tried to knock the puck into the goal. Just as her stick was about to hit the puck, though, Amka shot in front of her, intercepted it, and passed it to Sam.

He wobbled on his skates but managed to stop the puck with his stick. Then he turned and took off toward the opposite goal, pushing the puck back and forth on the ground in front of him.

"I'm open!" yelled one of Sam's teammates, who was wearing bright yellow skates. Sam attempted to pass it to her, but before he could, another player much taller than Sam swooped in and swiped the puck, passing it to Scott.

Sam let out a defeated sigh, but Amka rolled up next to him and clicked her hockey stick against his. "You're doing great," she said. "Just remember to *reach*!"

Sam caught his breath and nodded. "Okay," he said, huffing. "Yes! Okay. Reach."

Amka smiled as she took off after the puck, Sam close behind her.

Sam watched from the center of the road as Scott passed the puck back to the tall player. *Reach*, Sam thought to himself, and he pushed off from the ground and raced on.

As he rolled toward the tall player, he held out his hockey stick and stretched toward the puck. Before the player could react, Sam intercepted the puck and skated away. He quickly passed the puck to Amka, who scooped it up and lined up her shot. Both Scott and Sofia were zooming toward her.

"Shoot!" someone cried.

"Shoot!" Sam echoed.

And with a quick arc of her shoulder, Amka hit the puck right into the opposing team's net.

"GOOOAAAAL!" yelled the player with the yellow skates.

"Yes! You did it!" Sam said to Amka, beaming with pride.

"No, *we* did it!" she responded.

All of the players rolled toward them and brought their sticks together in a celebratory cheer.

"Nice shot!" Scott said to Amka.

"Good game," Sofia agreed, beaming.

Scott smiled at Sofia. "You're a natural on those skates," he said. "You should come play with us again."

"I'd love to," Sofia grinned. "Whenever we're in town. What do you say, Amka? Rematch?"

"Definitely!" Amka said. "Rematch for sure."

Soon the players began to roll off, waving their

goodbyes and leaving Sam, Sofia, and Amka in front of Amka's house, where they sat on the front step with some water bottles.

"So," Amka said, pulling off her skates, "tell me your story. How'd you two get here so fast? Didn't your aunt just get home?"

Sam nodded as he tied his sneakers. "She did. But we got so excited about the grove in your letter," he said, "we had to come see you. Remember how you said you wished you had a way to look for it?"

"Sure," Amka said, lacing up her own sneakers.

"Well," Sam said, "we have something to show you."

Amka slung her backpack over her shoulders as the three walked over to the scooter. Sam watched Amka's face closely as he and Sofia explained the technology housed within the scooter's touch screen. He knew it was a lot to digest, and he'd seen friends in the past react in different ways. Would she believe them? Would she think they were making a joke? He wasn't sure what she would do, and it took Sam by surprise when she walked around the scooter in a circle and put her hand on its seat.

"Show me what it can do," she said, then tightened her backpack straps.

"Really?" asked Sofia.

"The only way I'm going to believe you is if you prove it," she said.

"That can be arranged," Sam said, exchanging a glance with Sofia. "Where should we go?"

"It can go anywhere?" Amka asked.

Sam nodded. "Anywhere."

"If you were going to search for the Forgotten Grove of Fire," Sofia said, "where would you start?"

"I have no idea," Amka said. Then her face lit up. "But I know someone who does."

The three climbed onto the scooter, and Sam entered the destination.

"Hold on tight, okay?"

Amka didn't seem convinced anything was about to happen. "Sure," she said skeptically.

Whiz . . . Zoom . . . FOOP!

3

An Excessive
Collection of Cats

hen Sam opened his eyes, Amka was already off the scooter and pacing back and forth, her ponytail whipping from side to side as she walked.

"I can't believe this!" she said. "We were at my house—and then we—" She stopped in her tracks and turned to Sam and Sofia. "You do this all the time?"

"If you had the scooter," Sofia said, "wouldn't you? I mean, look at this!"

Sam turned to see Sofia's view of the city. The scooter had dropped them on a road at the top of a small hill, and in the distance, tall buildings reached into the sky alongside glistening tree-framed waterways. Cars motored down winding streets with bikers and pedestrians moving about on either side.

"Welcome to Montreal," Amka said. She shook her head, looking out at the view. "I can't believe we're here."

"Want to know what *I* believe?" Sam asked. "I believe the scooter can help us find the Forgotten Grove of Fire."

Amka's eyes grew wide. "Let's do it!"

Sofia jumped with excitement. "Okay," she said. "Who are we here to see?"

After parking the scooter, Sam and Sofia followed Amka to the front door of a house that looked like a log cabin. Amka knocked, and soon after an older woman with gray-streaked hair and a warm, friendly face answered. Something about her instantly reminded Sam and Sofia of Amka. When the woman's eyes landed on Amka, she smiled with joy.

"My love!" the woman cried. "It can't be!" She squinted her eyes with her hands on her hips. "Is this another one of your surprises? What a delight! I didn't know you were coming."

The woman stepped forward and pulled Amka

into a hug.

"Hi, Grandma," Amka said, stepping back but still holding her grandmother's hands. "These are my friends Sam and Sofia. Sam and Sofia, this is my grandmother Adjiukak."

"You can call me Grandma Adji." She smiled a smile so sweet, Sam instantly felt at home. "Your aunt Charlie told me all about you."

"And who is this?" Sofia said, bending down to greet a puffy gray Siberian cat that appeared at Grandma Adji's feet.

"This is Garnet," Grandma Adji said. "Garnet, get back inside, sweet thing. It's too cold for you out here today."

Garnet looked up at Sam, unblinking.

"Uh, hello," Sam said.

Garnet meowed in response as Sofia reached out to pet her head.

"Speaking of which, come inside, you three," Grandma Adji said, motioning them in. "Come out of the chill. And have something to eat!"

Sam and Sofia followed Amka in, the sounds of laughter and music surrounding them as they paused to take off their shoes. Sam set his sneakers next to Amka's backpack along the wall, and when he leaned over, another cat, this one small and white, slunk past him, brushing him with its tail.

"You arrived just in time," Grandma Adji said. "We're just sitting down to an early dinner."

Sam followed the woman down the hall. He didn't know where to look first. The house was filled with paintings and photographs of forests and lakes, small animal carvings, stone sculptures, and colorful tapestries made of interwoven fabric, thread, and feathers. Sam also noticed clusters of sparkling crystals, more plants than he could count, and, most noticeably,

an excessive collection of cats.

Garnet had been following Sam closely since they'd entered the house, purring, meowing, and flicking her tail. As Sam moved through the hall, she wove playfully through his legs. From every corner and atop each piece of furniture, there seemed to be another cat blinking at him. Small cats, large cats, young cats and old; orange tabbies and brown mountains of fur—Sam was glad he wasn't allergic!

Grandma Adji led the three of them to her dining room, which was beautifully decorated with more mementos and keepsakes. Sitting around the table were a

small group of Grandma Adji's friends.

The two making the most noise—laughing loudly at some old pictures—were Nilo and Aras Martin, a pair of identical twins, both about Aunt Charlie's age, with beards carefully trimmed into points at their  chins. Across from them sat Gwen, a petite woman with brown hair that framed her face in soft curls. She smiled and pulled out the chairs on either side of her as the kids entered the room.

From another doorway came a cheerful man carrying a tray of fish covered in bright medallions of lemon. His name was River, and he wore an apron over a long, cozy cardigan sweater.

"Welcome!" he said. "I hope you like fish." He motioned for the kids to sit at the table, which they did, Sam suddenly hungry thanks to the appetizing smells wafting up in front of him.

As Grandma Adji introduced everyone, the twins started serving up fresh vegetables, split pea soup, a cheesy Canadian French fry dish called poutine, and, of course, River's freshly roasted fish. Everything was delicious—the kind of food that warms your soul.

Hanging on a far wall was a painting of a sparkling night sky. Green and blue brushstrokes swirled over a grove of pine trees like a cluster of shimmering clouds.

"Your art is so beautiful," Sam told Grandma Adji.

"Thank you, dear," Grandma Adji said. She followed Sam's gaze and nodded at the painting. "The aurora borealis," she said. "One of our planet's most stunning natural wonders. Aren't the northern lights magical?"

"If you're in the right place at the right time," Nilo added, "you might catch a glimpse of them while you're here in Canada."

"It's a spiritual experience for many Inuit people," Aras said.

"Have you ever seen them?" Sofia asked.

Grandma Adji nodded. "A few times when I was a girl, and again a couple of years back."

"I haven't seen them yet," Amka said, staring wistfully at the painted swirls of color across the room.

"You will one day, my love," said Grandma Adji, "and when you do, you'll cherish the memory forever. The painting helps me do exactly that.

I have so many cherished memories," she added, waving a hand around the room, "so I pack the house full of art to remind me of them every day."

"And plants!" Sofia said. "You have so many different kinds, I can't decide which is my favorite."

"She's been collecting them for years," Amka said, reaching for more vegetables.

"River and I can't resist a beautiful plant," Grandma Adji said. "He's really the one with the green thumb."

"I don't see it," said Sam.

River chuckled. "It's just an expression," he said, wiggling his thumbs. "It means you have a talent for gardening and tending to plants."

"Art and nature are precious to the Inuit people," Amka said.

"Indeed they are,"

Gwen said.

"Our families," Grandma Adji said, "have lived here in Canada and Alaska for centuries."

"And Greenland!" Nilo added.

Grandma Adji smiled. "Greenland too," she said. "Before this land was colonized by settlers, indigenous people called the rivers and lakes and mountains their home. We remember our ancestors and keep their traditions alive through art and music and food." She motioned to the spread in front of them.

As if on cue, Garnet jumped onto Sam's lap, snagged the rest of the fish from his plate, then dashed down the hall.

"And our love of animals and nature!" River added.

Everyone around the table laughed, and Gwen

put another piece of fish on Sam's plate. Sam looked around the room at the other felines. A small tabby sat high up on a far bookshelf, reminding Sam of the cat he'd seen on the fence back home.

"They sure do climb everything, don't they?" Sam said.

Gwen glanced up at the tabby on the shelf. "This one gets nervous around strangers, and cats instinctively look for high ground when they are afraid."

"Nothing to be scared of, little one," Sofia said, and Grandma Adji smiled.

"What can I say?" Grandma Adji said. "Animals have my heart. I've had cats since I was a girl.

 We used to follow them through the forest on our little childhood adventures."

Amka looked quickly at Sam and Sofia. "Your adventures looking for the Forgotten Grove of Fire, you mean?" Amka asked.

Grandma Adji laughed. "I certainly did my share of looking. I was always mesmerized by that story. I've told *you* all, I'm sure." She looked at her friends around the table, who all nodded.

"The famous grove," Gwen said, "of course."

"Has Amka told you the tale?" River asked, and Sam and Sofia nodded.

"It sounds like such a special place," Sofia said.

Grandma Adji sat for a moment, lost in thought as the others finished their meals. "You know," she finally said, "my great-grandfather was the last person in our family to find the grove, even though many have tried to find it. Do you remember the clues?" she asked Amka.

"Of course," Amka said.

"I wrote down in my notebook what you said in your letter, Amka," Sofia added.

"Will you read it to us?" River asked.

"Yes, refresh our memories," said Nilo.

Sofia pulled out her notebook, found the page, and began reading aloud to the group: "Follow the purple footprints from the mouth of the bear. The path will be hidden beyond the Emerald Door, an entrance next to the farthest-reaching hand and visible only by the strongest light. There lie the green flames that sing the sky's song: the Forgotten Grove of Fire."

"What a beautifully written mystery," Silas said.

"Do you know what the riddle means, Grandma?" Amka asked.

"Not exactly," Grandma Adji replied, and Sam's heart sank.

Follow the purple foot-
prints from the mouth of
the bear. The path will be
hidden beyond the
Emerald Door, an
entrance next to the
farthest-reaching hand
and visible only by the
strongest light. There lie
the green flames that
sing the sky's song: the
Forgotten Grove of Fire.

Maybe the scooter wasn't enough to find the grove after all.

But then, Grandma Adji smiled. "I can give you a hint, though." She turned to her friends. "You all wouldn't mind if I took the kids on a little walk, would you?"

"Of course not," Gwen said.

"We have each other—and plenty of cats—for company," added River.

"Wonderful!" Grandma Adji stood from the table. She looked at Amka, Sofia, and Sam one by one. "Follow me."

4

Meeting Mother Earth

Sam, Sofia, and Amka followed Grandma Adji from the house into the brisk Montreal air. After a short walk, they'd left the quaint homes of Grandma Adji's street and stepped into a busier part of the neighborhood, where they weren't the only ones out for a walk. People bustled by, ducking into brick apartment buildings, shops, and other businesses. Cars motored along the road and the occasional bike rolled past with the chime of a handlebar bell.

Sam tilted his head back as the buildings became larger, some reaching tall above them, their windows glistening in the sun. That's when he noticed a sign on a nearby door reading *La Petite Boulangerie.*

"Is that French?" Sam asked.

"*Oui!*" Amka answered. "Yes, I think it means *The Little Bakery*?" She looked to her grandmother.

"That's right, Amka," Grandma Adji said. "French is the official language of Quebec, and Montreal is one of the most bilingual cities in Canada."

"I didn't know that!" Sofia said.

"Our family also speaks Inuktitut," said

Grandma Adji, "the indigenous language of the Inuit. Oh—here we are!"

The group found themselves approaching a small crowd gathered around a long fountain. Its clear waters led to a grand stone building surrounded by plants. Grandma Adji motioned to a banner set up along the pathway. The letters spelled out words in both French and English: *Bienvenue au Jardin Botanique de Montréal – Welcome to the Montreal Botanical Garden.*

"This is one of my favorite places in town," Grandma Adji said. "It's one of the reasons I bought the house. Just a few minutes of walking and here you are."

"How do you say 'welcome' in Inuktitut?" Sofia asked.

"*Atelihai!*" Amka said, spreading her arms toward the entrance.

Once inside, Grandma Adji led the trio to the center of the garden, a beautiful space full of plants and flowers. Sam gasped when he caught sight of a green sculpture rising from the ground. A collection of lush leaves, vines, and blossoms formed the shape of a larger-than-life woman reaching up from the ground, a waterfall of plants cascading from her hand. They paused in front of her, as if stopping to say hello.

"She's beautiful," Sofia said in a whisper.

"She represents Mother Earth," Amka said.

"She looks like old pictures of my mom," Sofia said, and Sam agreed. Something about the shape of Mother Earth's cheeks reminded him of Mama Lyla. He raised his camera for a group picture.

As they continued on their way, they passed small lakes and waterways, courtyards and canopies, and more sculptures, including an old car completely covered in leaves and vines. Finally, Grandma Adji stopped in an area full of hundreds of Canadian flowers. The native blooms grew together to form a living painting.

Sofia pointed to an orange flower with markings that looked like cheetah spots. "Is that a lily?"

Grandma Adji smiled. "You're absolutely right."

"I recognize it from Aunt Charlie's photos. And look!" Sofia hurried over to a cluster of yellow flowers. "Okanagan sunflowers! Just like the ones I potted back home."

Sam spotted a strangely shaped pink flower. "Does anyone know what this one is called?"

"I think that's a lady's slipper," Amka answered.

Grandma Adji nodded in agreement. "You know your flowers. Some of these grow throughout North America, and some grow just in Canada. Amka, our Inuit ancestors enjoyed these same flowers years and years ago."

"I love coming here with you," Amka said. Then a question washed over her face. "But, Grandma, why did you bring us here today? What do these flowers have to do with the story of the grove?"

"Ah, yes," Grandma Adji said. "The Forgotten Grove of Fire." She stepped in front of a large cluster of vibrant purple flowers. These weren't like the purple saxifrage Sam had planted at home. Though a similar purple shade, these blooms grew in thin stalks, standing in straight violet plumes that moved delicately in the wind.

"I still don't know where the grove is," Grandma Adji said, "but that doesn't mean you won't find it, my dear." She put her hands on Amka's shoulders and looked her in the eyes. "Part of the journey, Great-Grandpa always said, is discovering the way for yourself."

Sam held his breath, waiting for what Grandma Adji would say next. He had a feeling she knew more than she was letting on.

"When I was young," she continued, "something unexpected marked the pathway home from our days playing in the forest." She caught Sam's eye. "Something purple." She turned to the flowers dancing in the breeze.

The three friends looked at each other in realization. "The purple footprints!" they said in unison.

"We called it willowherb," Grandma Adji told them, motioning to the flowers. "Legend has it, these same purple footprints will lead lucky visitors to the Forgotten Grove of Fire." They all stared at the willowherb, and Sam lifted his camera and took a picture of the purple blossoms.

Click-click!

"The only problem?" Grandma Adji added. "The area where we used to live with my great-grandfather is *very* far from here, all the way up in the Northern Territory." She took one last wistful look at the willowherb. "One day we'll visit, Amka."

Grandma Adji gave Amka a kiss on the forehead and wandered back toward Mother Earth. "And if you're looking for the mouth of the bear," she said over her shoulder, "a map might be helpful." She turned and gave Amka's arm a squeeze. "You know how much our family loves to camp." And she continued down the path, disappearing into the garden.

Amka turned to Sam and Sofia with wide, excited eyes. "I know where to go!"

5

The Mouth of the Bear

After some goodbye hugs, Sam, Sofia, and Amka huddled around the scooter still parked outside of Grandma Adji's house. Sam pulled up a map of Canada's Northern Territory on the touch screen and let Amka zoom in to enlarge a specific area.

"They only took me camping there a few times," Amka said as she tapped around on the map, "but it has to be the right place. It *has* to be." She leaned forward, her nose almost brushing the screen, then pulled back. "There! Found it."

All at once, the three climbed onto the scooter.

"Hold on!" Sam said.

"You don't have to tell me twice," Amka said, clutching the seat tightly.

"*Vamos!*" Sofia said.

Whiz . . . Zoom . . . FOOP!

Sam opened his eyes and craned his neck back. They were now surrounded by lush forest at the shore of a wide lake. The trees here were taller than any he'd seen in Compass Court, their trunks reaching up into the darkening sky, disappearing into shadow.

Amka took the backpack off her shoulder and hung it on one of the scooter's handlebars as she blinked to adjust her eyes.

"Yes!" she said, peering around. "This is where we used to camp. It's called Great Bear Lake."

Sam spun around to face her. "Did you say 'bear'?" he asked. "You think this is the mouth of the bear from the story?"

Dimples appeared on Amka's cheeks as she nodded, eyes glinting with excitement.

Sam watched as Sofia, still sitting on the scooter, tapped the touch screen. "If you use your imagination, you can see how this part of the lake kind of looks like the head of a bear, and this campsite," she said, "is at the bear's mouth!"

"Now we just need to find the purple footsteps," said Amka.

"Willowherb could be growing anywhere," Sam said. "We better start looking. The sun is about to set."

Sofia hopped up from the scooter and lifted the seat, revealing the storage compartment beneath. She pulled Sam's bag from inside and passed it to him. He flipped the top flap open and grabbed three flashlights, handing one each to Sofia and Amka. Sam clicked his on along with the others, the three sending beams of white light into their shadowy surroundings. Sam strapped the bag to his back.

"Let's start our search over there," Amka said. "That's where the lake forms the mouth of the bear."

"Great idea," Sofia said.

But before they could set off toward the shore, a scratching noise pulled Sam's attention back toward the scooter.

"What was *that*?" Amka asked, whipping her head toward the sound.

Sam pointed his light at the scooter, and the scratching got even louder.

"Look!" Sofia said. "Amka, your bag is moving!"

Sam moved his light to the backpack hanging from one of the handlebars, and sure enough, it was rocking from side to side in the air.

Sam inched closer.

"Be careful!" Amka whispered.

6

Following the Footsteps

Sam imagined Grandma Adji here at the lake as a child hunting for the Grove of Fire, and the thought gave him courage. He took another step closer to the scooter, and just as he reached out to open Amka's bag, out leapt Garnet the cat.

Sam dropped his flashlight as Garnet flew into his arms in a flash of gray fur.

"You rascal!" exclaimed Amka. "How'd you get in there?"

Sam could feel Garnet scrambling around in his arms, trying to find her footing. Then, suddenly, she let out a loud meow and jumped to the ground, racing off into the dark.

"Wait!" Sam cried, scooping up his flashlight. "Come back!"

Amka almost grabbed her, but Garnet was too quick. She darted past Amka and ran toward the trees. The three chased after her. It was almost completely dark now, and Sam could only

catch glimpses of Garnet's tail as she darted in and out of their flashlight beams. He was so worried about Garnet that it took him a minute to notice something purple at his feet. Many somethings.

"The purple footprints!" Sofia exclaimed.

"We barely had to look," Amka said in disbelief. "They're right here!"

Clusters of willowherb grew in thick patches, forming a pathway through the trees. Garnet wove between two large clusters, then darted down the path.

"She went left!" Sam called to the others.

"Follow her!" Amka cried.

Sam ran onward, sweeping his light from side to side. The three hunted through the dark, catching occasional glimpses of Garnet here and there. They came close to catching her a few times, but she was a stubborn little thing, and deeper along the path she went, zigging and zagging through the trees. Finally, Sam spotted her as she hopped atop the trunk of a fallen tree stretching over the running water of a creek about 10 feet below.

"Don't you dare cross that log," Sam said to Garnet. In response, the mischievous cat meowed, flicked her tail, and scurried effortlessly

across the trunk. Sam pointed his light and, on the other side of the creek, he could see more willowherb.

Sam stepped up onto the trunk as Sofia and Amka caught up to him. The frosty mountain air chilled his face, and he knew the water below was icy cold. He took a deep breath and steadied himself, taking a step forward before a quiet "Wait!" reached his ears.

Sam turned to see Amka nervously clutching her flashlight. "I don't think I can do it," she said. "I'm, uh, kind of afraid of heights."

"That's okay," Sofia said. "We'll find another way around."

"There's no time!" Amka said. "We'll lose Garnet."

Sam stepped down from the log and grabbed Amka's hand. "What if we do it together?"

Amka looked at him, her face aglow from her flashlight, and gave a half smile. "Okay," she said.

"I can do this."

Sam stepped back up onto the log. "Hold onto my back," he said.

Amka stepped up behind him and placed her hand on his shoulder.

Sam moved forward and heard Sofia step up and join them in the rear.

"I'm right behind you," he heard Sofia say.

"I'm okay," Amka said. "Go ahead. We can't lose her!"

Sam walked carefully along the log, moving over the creek.

"My family has lived among these trees for hundreds of years," Sam heard Amka say to herself. "This is my land. This is my home." Sam took another step, and another. "My ancestors walked this forest for me," Amka continued, and her voice was steady and powerful. Sam listened to each word, letting her voice lead him. "This tree fell to lead our way," Amka said. "These flowers grew for us." Sam stepped forward, the end of the log now in view. "Garnet is waiting for us. The Forgotten Grove of Fire is waiting for us." Sam shuffled onward. "Because we haven't forgotten. We will never forget where we come from."

"Almost there," Sam said. With another step, he hopped down from the log and grabbed Amka's hand as she ran the last few steps to safety with Sofia right behind.

"You did it!" Sofia said.

"No, *we* did it," Amka said, gasping for breath. "Thank you."

"Don't thank us too soon," Sam said, turning around.

On the other side of the creek, directly in front of them, a giant mountain wall stretched tall and wide, blocking their way.

"Oh no," Sofia said. "A dead end."

Amka pressed her hands against the wall of

rock. "Where could Garnet have gone?" she asked. "It's not safe for her out here!"

7

A Lucky Ledge

Sam scanned the cliffside with his flashlight. "We'll find her," he said, looking at the solid trunks growing up along the great mountain wall.

They followed the beam of light with their eyes

as it swept across the rock face, but saw nothing. Finally, up in the branches of a large spruce tree growing near the cliff wall, the reflective light from two small eyes grabbed Sam's attention.

"Garnet!" Sam shouted. "What are you doing up there, girl?"

"She must be afraid," said Sofia. "Gwen said that cats try to get higher when they're scared."

"That's the opposite of what I do," Amka said.

Sam watched as Garnet continued to climb the tree. Without a second thought, he tucked his flashlight into his bag and started climbing after her.

"Be careful, Sam!" Sofia called after him.

But Sam couldn't respond. He was moving so fast, he was already out of breath. He grabbed branch after branch, pulling himself up, finding whatever ledge or knob of bark he could step on, and with each motion, he got closer to the top of the tree line, surrounded by the dense foliage.

"He's coming for you, Garnet!" Amka's voice called up from below. "Stay put!"

When Sam finally reached the top of the tree, there was Garnet, holding tight to a branch with her claws. Sam inched closer, and that's when he noticed Garnet's branch was one of five that extended far from the trunk of the tree, which towered over the others around it, and was framed by the wall of stone. Sam squinted in the darkness, peering out at the five strong branches, and that's when it clicked in his mind: the hand from the family folktale! *What if the "hand" that's "reaching" isn't*

an actual hand, but something that looks like a hand? Sam thought.

"The reaching hand," Sam shouted down. "I think it's this tree! It's taller than any other tree around!"

Down on the forest floor, Sam heard Sofia yell, "It's too dark! We can't see anything down here."

Garnet let out a meow.

"It's okay, girl," Sam said softly.

He scooted along the branch, clutching it with all his strength. Keeping himself steady with one arm, he pulled the flashlight from his bag and inched closer to Garnet. Her eyes flashed nervously in the light before she let out a squeak and scurried forward, hopping onto Sam's shoulders.

"Gotcha!" Sam said. He tipped his head down. "I have her! Wait. What's that?" Sam adjusted the aim of his flashlight. Down below, along the cliff wall, Sam caught a glimpse of a sudden flash

of green.

"Can you two see what I'm seeing?" Sam called from his perch in the tree. Garnet purred in his ear in response.

"We need more light," Amka called up. "Can you get closer from where you are?"

Sam looked around him. The branches were thick—so thick, he wasn't quite sure how he'd squeezed through them so quickly. He didn't know how to break through the foliage, but he was determined. He repositioned himself and stretched out his arm, suddenly remembering Amka's hockey tip: *the stick is an extension of your arm.*

Sam took a deep breath. "Hold on, Garnet." He stretched along the branch and twisted his shoulder, using it to push the pine needles aside. With the parting of the needles, a path cleared in the branches. Sam aimed the flashlight at a section of the rock wall above Sofia and Amka. As his light joined each of theirs, Sam could see a ledge just above the girls' heads leading to what looked like another pathway.

"I think the grove is close," he called. "There's a ledge. You see it?"

Sam felt Garnet shift on his back. He thought the cat was slipping, but then she jumped gracefully from his shoulders onto a tree limb hanging near the top of the cliff. Then she leapt from the branch to the ledge, perching there as if waiting for them to follow.

"Garnet!" Amka cried from below. "Thank goodness you're okay!"

Sofia pointed at the cat. "You stay right there."

"I can lead you up," Sam called. "It's not that high. Just follow my light." He pointed his flashlight at a notch in the rock wall that he hadn't seen from below. "This spot looks stable. Can you reach it?"

He watched as Sofia lifted her arms toward the light and grabbed the handhold. Sam moved the light to a notch in the rock near her feet.

"Now step up there," Sam said.

Sofia put her foot where Sam's light shone and continued to follow his instructions until, pressing her foot against the same branch Garnet had used, she hopped up to the ledge where Garnet sat waiting.

Sam moved the light back to the handhold. "You got this, Amka!"

"Oh, I know," Amka answered. "After crossing that log, I can do anything."

She followed Sam's light, repeated Sofia's steps, and in a moment, she was up on the ledge too, holding Garnet in her arms.

His friends safe, Sam released the branch,

closing the gap with a shush of needles. Then he climbed down to the overhanging branch, eased out toward the ledge, and jumped over. Sofia pulled him in and away from the edge.

"Nice climbing," she said.

Amka hugged Sam so tightly she squeezed the air out of him. "Thank you!" she said. Garnet meowed. "She thanks you too."

Sam laughed, but Garnet kept meowing again and again, and when no one moved, she sprang from Amka's arms and ran along the ledge, taking a turn around a small boulder.

Amka hurried after her. "Why do you keep running away?!"

Sam and Sofia followed Amka, shining their lights as they went, to find Garnet crouching at the base of a large hump of rock. When their beams landed on it, brilliant dazzles of green glittered back at them. Sam couldn't believe his eyes. The rock was studded with countless

glimmering green shards.

Amka gasped as Garnet gave a pleased meow. "The Emerald Door," she said quietly. "We found it!"

8

Through the Emerald Door

Sam immediately took a picture: **Click-click!**

"It's more incredible than I ever imagined," he said.

He tucked his camera back in his bag, and when he turned back to the Emerald Door, Garnet was pawing at the ground in front of it.

"There's a tunnel!" Amka said, pointing, and sure enough, below the glints of green, the rock opened to reveal a small alcove curving into the

mountainside in a dark, jagged tube. Garnet blinked up at them, and dashed into the tunnel, a soft meow inviting them onward.

Amka smiled at her new friends. "Follow me," she said. Then she headed into the tunnel after Garnet.

Sofia went in second, followed by Sam, each of them doing their best to illuminate the way with their flashlights as they inched along the narrow space. Emerald green chunks were imbedded in the tunnel walls, their reflected light giving the passage an eerie glow.

Sam stopped for a moment to look at his hands under the flickering green light. "I guess you can say I have a green thumb now too," he said, and Sofia and Amka's laughs echoed through the tunnel.

Suddenly, Sofia stopped in front of Sam.

Amka called back, "I think I see a glow up ahead. Turn off your flashlights."

"You got it," said Sofia.

Each of them clicked off their lights. Sam blinked, trying to get used to the near-complete dark, and after a moment, he saw a hazy light in the distance.

"It's up ahead," Amka said.

"*Vamos!*" said Sofia.

Sam followed Sofia, scooting along the tight crevice little by little.

"We're almost there," called Amka.

Finally, Sofia pulled herself out of the tunnel, and Sam followed right behind. When he emerged from the rock, he stopped and stared in amazement.

9

The Forgotten
Grove of Fire

am's jaw dropped as Amka sucked in a
deep breath and Sofia let out a whispered
"Wow!" Even the cat, once a ball of energy, sat
still as a statue, staring up.

Before them was a large clearing etched into the mountainside, the ground covered entirely with purple willowherb blooms, and above, brilliant wisps of the aurora borealis streamed through the sky like a multicolored river. The shimmering ropes danced above them in dazzling greens, blues, and yellows.

"We did it," Sofia whispered.

"This is it," said Amka, tears filling her eyes. "The Forgotten Grove of Fire." Garnet hopped into her arms, purring happily.

Sam tipped his head back to take in the glorious fire in the sky as the purple flowers swayed around him.

"I should have known the grove would lead to the northern lights," Amka said.

"I guess you'll need to get a painting of your own now," Sofia said, "to remember this moment."

"I guess I do!" Amka said. She shook her head in awe. "But I can't imagine how I'd ever forget."

Sam turned to take in the wonder of the space. A steep wall rose into the sky behind them, overgrown with shrubs and trees except for the small tunnel opening. The rock face rose higher than Sam's flashlight beam could reach, blocking the grove from the forest around them and framing the sky in a massive hoop, as if the grove were a stage made specially to hold the fiery lights above them.

"No wonder this is so hard to find," Sam said. "The mountains almost completely block the sky."

After a long while quietly looking up at the northern lights, Sam finally pulled the camera from his bag again. "May I?" he asked Amka.

She nodded with a smile. "Grandma Adji won't believe it," she said. "I'll need the pictures for proof!"

Sam started taking photos—**Click-click!**—as Sofia and Amka began surveying the willowherb flowers surrounding them.

"I just realized," Sofia said, "I don't recognize these from Aunt Charlie's photos."

"I wonder…" Sam said, realization creeping in. "There was one flower that Aunt Charlie couldn't find on her trip," he told Amka, "called fireweed. She was really disappointed she missed it. It's purple."

"Like purple saxifrage," Sofia said. "But taller."

"And skinnier," Sam said, eyeing the thin stalks of the willowherb.

"Could willowherb and fireweed be the same flower?" Sofia asked.

Sam's chest tingled with excitement. "It could be!"

"Even if it isn't fireweed," Amka said, "maybe she'd like to add another purple flower to her studies." Amka plucked a willowherb stalk from the ground and handed it to Sam.

"Thank you," he said, touched. Sam found a

spare bandanna from his bag and gently wrapped the flower in its cloth. He tucked the bundle back in the bag and smiled. "Let's take a selfie," he said. He held up his camera as the three gathered around. "Say willowherb!"

"Willowherb!" Sofia and Amka said together.

Click-click!

"I hate to say it," Sofia said, "but we should probably head home soon." Sam knew she was right. Sofia was spending the night at Sam's house, and they needed to get ready for bed soon.

"My parents will be wondering where I am too," Amka agreed.

The three looked at one another. "Maybe just a while longer?" Sam suggested, and Amka nodded.

"Just a little," she said, and the friends gazed up into the sky, basking in the glow of the lights.

10

The Folktale Flower

Whiz . . . Zoom . . .
FOOP!

Aunt Charlie opened the door to the garage
moments after Sam and Sofia had slid into their
sleeping bags. Sam could still hear the hum of

the scooter's engine cooling down as he smiled innocently at his aunt.

"You sure you two want to sleep here in the lab?" she asked.

Sofia nodded as she plucked a pine needle out of Sam's hair.

"It's our favorite place," Sam said, looking up at the glowing stars stuck to the ceiling. "The perfect spot for a sleepover."

"It's not too late for a bedtime snack, is it?" Aunt Charlie revealed a plate from behind her back and set it on a small table between Sam and Sofia. On it sat a small pile of pastries covered in whipped cream.

"What are these?" asked Sofia as she snatched one up and took a bite.

"They're called beaver tails," Aunt Charlie said. "I didn't get the chance to have one while I was in Canada, so I decided to bake some. Amka's grandmother emailed me the recipe. They're made with cinnamon and sugar."

"Grandma Adji?" Sam asked, before thinking.

"Did I tell you her nickname?" Aunt Charlie asked.

Sam looked at Sofia, took a big bite of beaver tail, and shrugged.

"Maybe I forgot," Aunt Charlie said with a wink. "Don't stay up too late. We have more gardening to do tomorrow."

"That reminds me," Sam said, his mouth full of pastry, "we have something for you." He pulled the bandanna from his bag and handed it to Aunt Charlie. She unwrapped the bandanna to reveal the purple willowherb blossom Amka had plucked. Aunt Charlie stared at the bloom in shock.

"It's called willowherb," Sofia said.

"But we think it might have another name too," Sam said.

"You're right about that," Aunt Charlie said. "The genus of this flower is called *Chamaenerion angustifolium*, also known as—"

"Fireweed!" Sam exclaimed.

Aunt Charlie nodded. "What a beautiful specimen!" she said, beaming.

"You'll never guess where we got it," Sam said, shooting a glance at Sofia.

Aunt Charlie smiled at her nephew. "I think I have an idea." Then she reached down and took a bite of her own pastry. "Maybe we should preserve this flower instead of trying to plant it. We could press it and frame it."

"You can do that?" Sofia asked, excited.

Aunt Charlie nodded. "Sure! I'll show you how tomorrow."

Just then, through the open door, the stray neighborhood cat padded into the garage, curled up beside Sam in a fuzzy black ball, and began purring happily.

"Where did *you* come from?" Sam asked, rubbing behind the cat's ear.

"I couldn't help it," Aunt Charlie said. "I saw her again and I had to feed her!"

"You found your way to the right house," Sam said to the cat.

"Maybe some purple footprints led her here," Sofia said with a giggle.

Sam smiled. Maybe they did. After today, he could believe anything.

Akumi
(The End)

Inuktitut Terms and Phrases

- **Atelihai** - Welcome

- **Halu** - Hello

- **Ilaali** - You're welcome

- **Kinauvit?** - What's your name?

- **Nakurmiik** - Thank you

- **Qanuipit?** - How are you?

- **Tavvauvusi** - Goodbye

- **Ulaatiakut** - Good morning

- **Unukattiakut** - Good evening

- **Ullukattiakut** - Good afternoon

French Terms and Phrases

- Au revoir - Goodbye

- Bienvenue au Jardin Botanique de Montréal - Welcome to the Montreal Botanical Garden

- La Petite Boulangerie - The little bakery

- Merci - Thank you

- Oui - Yes

- Salut - Hello

Portuguese Terms

- Papai - Dad

- Vamos! - Let's go!

Sofia and Sam's Snippets

The country of Canada is divided into 3 territories (the Northwest Territories, Nunavut, and the Yukon) and 10 provinces: Alberta, British Columbia, Manitoba, New Brunswick, Newfoundland and Labrador, Nova Scotia, Ontario, Prince Edward Island, Quebec, and Saskatchewan.

Whitehorse is the capital of the Yukon. The city is named after the white caps of the rapids in the Yukon River, which people thought looked like the manes of white horses.

The thriving wilderness of Canada's mountains and forests are filled with various animal species, including moose, beavers, wolves, bears, and wild cats. Every year, 200,000 porcupine caribou cross  the lands of the Yukon in one of the largest migrations of mammals in the world.

The aurora borealis (also called the northern lights) is an awe-inspiring natural phenomenon that creates rippling bursts of vibrant color in the sky. The shimmering lights are caused by particles from the Sun reacting with gases in Earth's atmosphere.

The type of molecules the particles collide with determine the colors of the northern lights. Oxygen molecules cause yellow and green light, and nitrogen molecules produce violet and blue.

Earth isn't the only planet in our solar system that experiences auroras. Astronomers have detected auroras on Jupiter, Saturn, Uranus, and Neptune.

Along with the First Nations and Métis communities, the Inuit are one of three distinct groups of indigenous Canadians who have called the country home for thousands of years. The word Inuit means "the people" in Inuktitut, the indigenous language of the Inuit.

The creation of art is an important and respected practice among Inuit communities, with genres including embroidery, tapestry, beading, sculpture, wood carving, and painting. The Inuit Art Foundation (IAF) supports and promotes the work of Inuit artists throughout Canada.

Maple syrup, now a popular food around the world, was first collected and enjoyed by indigenous peoples of Canada. After collection, the sap of maple trees was frozen and its top shell of ice was removed, separating the water from the concentrated sugar left behind in the remaining sap.

Of the 35 million or so people who live in Canada, about 10.4 million can speak French conversationally or fluently. Of Canada's 10 provinces, Quebec is the province with the highest concentration of French speakers.

Ice hockey is a winter sport played between two teams. Players use sticks to move and "shoot" a rubber disk called a puck into the opposing team's goal.

The sport of hockey is so popular in Canada, many children learn to ice skate not long after learning to walk. Canada has the largest number of ice hockey rinks in the world.

"Never Forget" Flower Press

Press and preserve your own flower clippings just like Sam, Sofia, and Aunt Charlie!

Materials:

- [ ] 1 piece of white paper
- [ ] 2 pieces of cardboard
- [ ] Fresh flowers, leaves, etc.
- [ ] 1 paper towel
- [ ] 3-5 heavy *books*

Details: About 10 minutes, not including pressing time

Instructions:

1. Place a sheet of white paper on top of one of the cardboard pieces.

2. Arrange your fresh flowers, leaves, and other plant parts on the piece of paper. Flatten thicker flowers with your hands to achieve the placement you'd like.

3. Place a paper towel on top of the paper, making sure to cover all of the flowers.

4. Place the second piece of cardboard on top of the paper towel to anchor the flowers in place.

5. Slip the cardboard stack into the center of a heavy book, like a dictionary, and set it aside in a safe place.

6. Stack two to four other books on top. The heavier, the better.

7. Over three to seven days, the heavy books will press the moisture from the flowers, flattening and preserving them. The waiting can be a challenge, but it's worth it!

8. Save and display the flowers in a small dish or picture frame to enjoy!